The
Colour Thief of Bristol

Philippa and Vicky Lilford

Alba and Evie are best friends.
They live in the colourful streets of
Montpelier, Bristol.

Alba and Evie are very naughty little
girls and they are always getting into
trouble for going on adventures.

Their favourite adventure is to
pretend they are world famous
detectives solving weird and
wonderful crimes around Bristol.

And it just so happened that one day,
there was a very weird and wonderful
crime indeed.

Alba and Evie love their school. Their headmistress, Miss Clement is full of fun. She wears colourful dresses, large dangly earrings and is always laughing.

Miss Clement makes sure their lessons are short and playtime is long. There is a large, colourful playground where they play for hours with their friends Margot, Imogen and Sadhya.

One day, Miss Clement is visited by a tall man dressed in a boring grey suit. The girls notice him because he looks very severe and, when he leaves, Miss Clement scowls at them all, which is very unlike her.

The next day Alba and Evie arrive at school and they are made to change into disgusting grey uniforms.

Evie notices that the playground has been removed and when they go inside all the colourful posters and pictures have been taken down to reveal boring white walls!

Miss Clement is talking sternly to the deputy headmistress Mrs Makena. They are both dressed in grey and rather than smiling at the children they shout at them and tell them off for laughing.

"What do you think you're doing out here girls?" shouts Miss Clement when she sees Evie, Alba and Margot in the playground.

"Get inside immediately!" She hisses.
"The playground is shut and you will be learning maths all day long".

After school, Alba and Evie walk up to St Andrew's park. "It's probably nothing to worry about" says Evie. "Everything will be back to normal tomorrow".

They see their friends Conor, Frankie and Mabel in the playground and join them.

"Why are you all looking so sad?" asks Alba.

"A horrible man came to our school today and made our teacher sad" says Frankie. Alba and Evie stare at each other.

"What do you mean?" Alba asks, horrified.

"He came to the school and afterwards our teachers were cross and gave us all detention" says Conor. "It was so unfair"

"Look!" shouts Mabel. "That's him!"

"Quick" Evie screams. "Let's follow him!"

Evie and Alba follow the mean looking man to Montpelier train station where they see their friend Callum.

"Callum, have you seen a tall man in a grey suit?" asks Evie.

"Yes," says Callum, "he's about to get on the train. Why?"

Alba and Evie quickly explain and Callum's eyes light up.

"This all sounds very fishy to me. But wait! I can help! I already know his name" shouts Callum. Evie and Alba turn to each other, surprised. "How can you know his name?" asks Alba, curiously.

"Saw it on his suitcase!" exclaims Callum.

"It's Mr G.Rumpy that you're after. And we'd better get on that train quickly or we'll lose him for good" Callum says, before clambering onto the train with Alba and Evie in tow.

Mr Rumpy gets off the train at Clifton Down Station and Callum, Evie and Alba follow him, trying their best to look inconspicuous.

After following him for a while, Mr Rumpy disappears behind the water tower on the Downs.

"That's strange" says Callum. "I can't see him anywhere".

Evie notices their friend Teddy working with his Dad hiring out hot air balloons. "Have you seen a tall man in a grey suit?" Evie asks Teddy.

But before Teddy can answer they hear Alba shouting.

"Oh no! Look" she screams, pointing into the sky. "That's Mr Rumpy up in that hot air balloon."

"We'll never find him now" says Evie looking upset. "I guess our school will be gloomy forever".

Alba and Evie start walking home, feeling glum.

"It's no good" wails Alba, "there's no way of finding him now".

As they are about to reach home, they bump into the three sisters, Issy, Beth and Emily. Evie notices they look sad too. "Let me guess, a man came to your school and now it's horrible there" she jests.

Issy, Beth and Emily look at each other, stunned.

"How could you know that?" they ask, suspiciously.

"So, he's been to your school too!" says Alba and looks at Evie with a gleam in her eye. "I might just have a plan".

Alba rushes home and gets a map of Bristol. She marks the three schools which have been hit so far. "Look!" says Evie, "It's a circle!"

"That's right," Alba says triumphantly. "Which means this school's next" and she points at the school their friend Charlie attends.

The next morning Alba and Evie get up early and instead of going to their school, they sneak into Charlie's school and hide in a cupboard overlooking the headmistress's classroom. The hours pass by and there is no sign of Mr Rumpy. Instead they see their friend Charlie being told off for throwing water balloons, which Evie and Alba think is pretty funny.

"He's never going to come" sighs Alba. And just as they are about to give up, there is a knock on the door. Miss Vim, the headmistress, opens the door to a tall man with angry, pointy features.

Alba and Evie gasp and peer out of the cupboard as Mr Rumpy marches into the classroom.

"Excuse me, sir", says Miss Vim, "can I help you with something?"

"Yes, indeed you can," sneers Mr Rumpy and he turns around and starts rummaging through his suitcase.

"Whatever is the meaning of this intrusion?" asks Miss Vim, looking worried.

"You'll see" comes a cruel sounding voice and in an instant Mr Rumpy turns around and attaches a peculiar looking electronic device to Miss Vim's head.

She goes limp and her face becomes sad. The colour seems to drain out of her into a large glass bottle which Mr Rumpy places into his suitcase.

Evie and Alba sit rooted to the spot as Mr Rumpy storms out of the classroom. "We have to follow him" says Evie anxiously, "he must be stopped".

They jump up and run out of the cupboard, much to Miss Vim's surprise. The girls see Mr Rumpy walking down the street and follow him to a large, Gothic looking house. Alba and Evie sneak around the back of the house and squeeze through a window into the cellar.

"Look!" gasps Evie, as they stare at hundreds of glass bottles on shelves, each containing wisps of different colour.

Suddenly, Mr Rumpy comes storming down the stairs. He moves so quickly that the girls do not have a chance to hide and when he sees them he drops his suitcase in surprise.

"Who are you?!" he demands.

"We go to one of the schools you ruined!" shouts Alba. Mr Rumpy grabs her hand and opens his suitcase.

"You children don't understand" he says "I bet you have parents who love you and you go to a nice school. Imagine if you grew up in an orphanage and any time you laughed you were beaten. I can't stand the sound of a children's playground" and with that he pulls out the scary looking contraption from his suitcase.

"Nooooo!" screams Evie and she pushes Alba out of the way as the device hits her head.

As Mr Rumpy starts sucking out Evie's warmth and love, he notices that the wisps of colour are overflowing.

The wisps fill the glass jar and pour out, floating towards Mr Rumpy.

As Evie's colour envelops Mr Rumpy, his features soften. He looks at Evie with a smile and a tear in his eye.

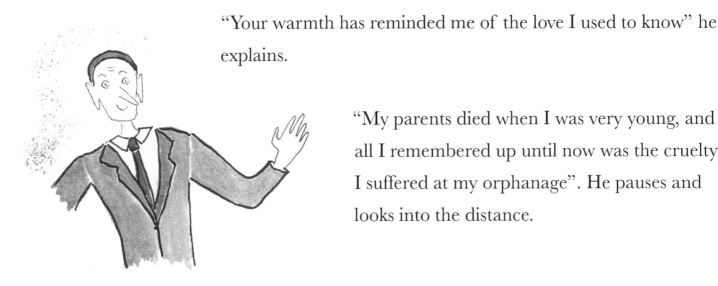

"Your warmth has reminded me of the love I used to know" he explains.

"My parents died when I was very young, and all I remembered up until now was the cruelty I suffered at my orphanage". He pauses and looks into the distance.

"But before that," Alba asks softly, "you had a nice mummy and daddy?"

"I did," says Mr Rumpy. "I had the kindest parents. I can hear my dad's laugh and my mum's singing again. Your love and warmth has helped to heal me. How can I thank you?"

"Is there any way of returning these people's colour?" asks Evie tentatively, pointing at the jars.

"Of course!" cries Mr Rumpy "and you girls must come with me."

So, Mr Rumpy, Alba and Evie collect up as many jars as they can and walk through Bristol, returning love to the colourful city.

First published in the United Kingdom in 2021 by
The Choir Press

ISBN 978-1-78963-232-3

Lightning Source UK Ltd.
Milton Keynes UK
UKHW050324070921
390122UK00006B/227